Mount Vernon's Magnificent Menagerie and the Very Mysterious Guest

Written by Linda Burgess

Illustrated by Maggie Dunlap

Mount Vernon Ladies' Association
Mount Vernon, Virginia

First Edition, 2012

Published in the United States by the
Mount Vernon Ladies' Association
Post Office Box 110
Mount Vernon, VA 22121

Library of Congress Cataloging-in-Publication Data

Burgess, Linda.
Mount Vernon's magnificent menagerie and the very mysterious guest / by Linda Burgess;
illustrated by Maggie Dunlap.—1st ed.
     p. cm.
Summary: Vulcan, a French foxhound belonging to General George Washington, asks the
many other animals of Mount Vernon what they have heard about the mysterious new
creature expected to arrive at the big party that night.
  ISBN 978-0-931917-31-8 (alk. paper)
[1. Animals—Fiction. 2. Mount Vernon (Va.: Estate)—Fiction.
3. Washington, George, 1732–1799—Family—Fiction. 4. Virginia—History—18th century—
Fiction.] I. Dunlap, Maggie, 1995– ill. II. Mount Vernon Ladies' Association. III. Title.
  PZ7.B916537Mou 2012
  [E]—dc23
                         2012016795

The efforts of the following staff members at George Washington's Mount Vernon Estate,
Museum, and Gardens were vital in creating this book:

Anne M. Johnson, Desktop Publishing Specialist
Susan Magill, Vice President for Advancement
F. Anderson Morse, Director for Development
Julia Mosley, Director of Retail
Mary V. Thompson, Research Historian

Book designer: Flynn Design, Groovinby, Ltd.
Managing editor: Stephen A. McLeod
Manuscript editor: Phil Freshman
Proofreaders: Phil Freshman and Stephen A. McLeod
Printed in China by Everbest through Four Colour Print Group

This book was typeset primarily in Mr. Peter and Mrs. Peter, with two complementary fonts,
Comenia Sans Condensed and Gros Marqueur.

Author's Note

Although this is a work of fiction, all the farm animals, pets, and people depicted on its pages once lived at Mount Vernon. Actual events that occurred at various times over a span of many years have been reimagined for the purpose of entertainment. Any laughter, delight, or interest in history derived from reading this story is purely intentional. —L. B.

Mount Vernon,
on the banks of the Potomac River,
was home to George and Martha
Washington for more than forty years.

George Washington was the first president of the United States of America. Although he was also a land surveyor, architect, successful businessman, and superb horseman, he mainly liked to think of himself as a farmer.

High on a hill overlooking a wide river, on an estate called Mount Vernon, there once lived a very famous farmer and his wife. This farmer was also a brave soldier who had led an army of his fellow citizens to victory in a long, hard war. For that reason, most people called him General. But to his wife, Martha Washington, he was George. Because they were so well known and so well liked, they were constantly opening their home to visitors.

Living with them at Mount Vernon were two of their grandchildren, Nelly and Washy. The children liked to turn cartwheels on the lawn and tumble down the hill to the deer park by the river. More than anything, Nelly and Washy loved to frolic with Mount Vernon's *menagerie*— which is a fancy way of saying a *caboodle of creatures.*

In 1785 the
Marquis de Lafayette,
who was one of General Washington's closest
friends, sent seven French foxhounds to Mount
Vernon—including Vulcan—as a gift.

Among this magnificent menagerie was a fine French foxhound named Vulcan. He was a handsome dog with a broad chest and a strong voice. Vulcan could run far and fast, and whenever the General took the hounds out for a chase, Vulcan led the pack. He lived with the other hounds in a large kennel that had a shed for shelter, a tree for shade, and a creek running through it with fresh, cool water.

One morning, the hounds were fast asleep, curled up and snug, when Rooster began to crow.

"Got-a-lot-to-do! Got-a-lot-to-do!"

Vulcan woke with a start and looked around.

"Got-a-lot-to-do! Got-a-lot-to-do!" Rooster stressed each syllable with a sense of urgency.

"Why are you waking us so early?" Vulcan asked. It wasn't even daylight yet.

"There is a party tonight. Lady Washington is bustling about the kitchen, and everyone's "got-a-lot-to-dooo!"

"So," Vulcan began thinking, "Lucy and Nathan are already cooking."

Vulcan loved parties, or *soirées*, as he would say in his native French. Most of all, he loved the tables full of food because that always meant leftovers for the hounds. He licked his lips. Vulcan could almost taste the savory feast scenting the morning air.

Lucy and Nathan
were cooks at Mount Vernon in the 1790s. They prepared breakfast, a large mid-afternoon dinner, and a light early-evening meal that was called "tea."

Two large dogs trotted past the kennel alongside Tom Davis, Mount Vernon's finest huntsman.

"Bonjour, Monsieur Pilot. Good day, Gunner," Vulcan called out to his fellow canines. "Have you heard about the *soirée* tonight?"

"Aye, laddie, we have," Pilot replied in his Irish brogue.

Gunner eagerly added, "I suppose you know we're expecting a very special guest."

Gunner and Pilot
were large, shaggy hunting dogs. Gunner was a Newfoundland. General Washington called Pilot his "water dog."

"Guest? No. Who? What? From where?" Vulcan asked.
"From some place far, far away," Pilot answered.
"Farther than France?" asked Vulcan.
"That's what we hear," said Gunner and Pilot.

Just then, General Washington rode up on his beloved horse Nelson. The hounds howled when the kennel gate swung open. Vulcan was the first to charge out. He led the pack across streams, over hills, and through thickets.

"Nelson, have you heard about the special guest coming to the party tonight?" Vulcan shouted to the large chestnut-colored steed.

Nelson whinnied. "I've heard it's strange and exotic."

Vulcan thought a moment. "Do you know how many legs it has?"

"No," said Nelson. "But Duke might. Ask him."

"Oh, I don't dare," Vulcan said.

Duke was an ornery old ox, and trespassing into his territory meant risking his wrath—and his horns.

After their run, the hounds filed back into the kennel for a big meal and a long nap. Vulcan slipped down to the stables instead. Perhaps someone there knew more about the mysterious foreigner.

Vulcan found Knight of Malta and Royal Gift in the paddock. The two donkeys were braying in fine harmony. Vulcan lapped a drink from their trough.

"Buenos días, Señor Vulcan," said the Spanish donkey, Royal Gift.

"Do you know about the unusual visitor coming tonight?" asked Vulcan.

"Sí, sí," said Royal Gift. "It has four legs, you know. I hope it's another donkey."

"I think it's too tall to be a donkey," said Knight of Malta. "Its hay crib is higher than we can reach. Maybe it's a mule."

"Or a draft horse," Royal Gift suggested. "In which case, the carriage dogs would know. Ask Sweetlips."

"Excellent idea," said Vulcan. Any excuse to talk to Sweetlips was a good one. Vulcan thought her quite beautiful, with her shiny white coat and reddish-brown spots.

The donkey **Royal Gift** was exactly that—a present to Washington from King Charles III of Spain. **Knight of Malta** was a donkey that came from France, courtesy of the Marquis de Lafayette.

Sweetlips was lounging in the midday sun with Captain and Madam Moose, the elder coach-hound couple. Vulcan rushed over and volunteered what he knew about the mystery guest.

"It's exotic, it has four legs, and the donkeys think it might be either a horse or mule," he explained.

"It can't be," Sweetlips said. "It has no hooves."

"Then it must have paws," Vulcan reasoned.

"That's the curiosity," Sweetlips said. "It doesn't have paws either."

"Then it has to have toes," Vulcan replied.

"Ask the house pets," said Sweetlips. "They're awfully good at eavesdropping."

Sweetlips, born in 1768, was a spotted hound that resembled a Dalmatian. As a "coach hound," she would run alongside carriages, helping keep passengers and their belongings safe.

In 1795 General Washington spent a dollar for a collar for Nelly's small pet spaniel, *Frisk*. *Pompey*, also a "little Spaniel dog," lived at Mount Vernon in 1768.

The Washingtons kept many kinds of birds at Mount Vernon. One of the most exotic was a *peacock*, purchased shortly after their wedding in 1759.

Vulcan loped off for the mansion, where the grandchildren were playing. Nelly was trying to teach the green parrot to speak, with little success. Washy played fetch with Pompey and Frisk, the two little spaniels, while the white cockatoo cocked its head and watched.

"What does anyone know about the special guest arriving tonight?" Vulcan asked.

"Not much," answered Mopsey, who'd been napping nearby.

Mopsey looked like a foxhound but wasn't quite as large as one. House dogs were generally smaller than working dogs, so they fit nicely on a person's lap. Mopsey normally liked to run and jump, but today she was acting sluggish and looking unusually plump.

"Aren't you feeling well?" Vulcan asked.

"I'm a little out of sorts," she answered. "It must have been something I ate. Probably the milk Washy spilled."

"More likely those scraps Nelly sneaks you under the table," Pompey added.

"I think I'll go inside and lie down." Mopsey waddled into the house, followed by her concerned friend Pompey.

Vulcan could not imagine eating right from the table. House pets sure had a comfortable life!

"The coach dogs tell me the guest has no hooves or paws," Vulcan continued. "Do you suppose it has toes?"

"What about feathers?" squawked Cockatoo. "Does it have feathers? We need more feathers around here."

"I bet it has wiry fur, like us," said one of the two feisty terriers. The other scampered about, nose to the ground, sniffing for rats.

"But I want it to have feathers!" Cockatoo cried. "For the sake of argument, let's just say it has feathers."

"Actually," Parrot interjected with authority, "it has a beard."

"A beard?!" shrieked Cockatoo. "Toes. Feathers. Beard. Wiry hair. What an odd-looking creature it must be."

"It has no feathers!" Parrot declared.

"But with feathers it could be an ostrich. No, wait. Turkeys have beards. That's it! It's a turkey!" Cockatoo exclaimed, with immense satisfaction.

In 1796 a pair of *terriers* lived at Mount Vernon. Their job was to help keep down the rodent population.

Unable to control himself, he leaped for the ham and sank his teeth into it. Lucy and Nathan, at work in the kitchen, turned as Vulcan raced for the door, the ham gripped in his jaws. Nathan dove for the dog as Lucy tried to grab the ham. But Vulcan was too swift. He scrambled out the door and disappeared deep into the woods.

When Washy later wrote about Vulcan's theft of the ham, he noted that George Washington laughed heartily at this "exploit" of his prized hound.

It was dark when laughter and lively music woke Vulcan from his nap. His belly was full, and his head was resting next to the enormous hambone, which had been picked clean. He sprang to his feet. The party had started without him! Vulcan took off like a flash for the mansion.

Suddenly, he stopped and pricked up his ears. The hounds were howling. He sniffed the air. SMOKE!

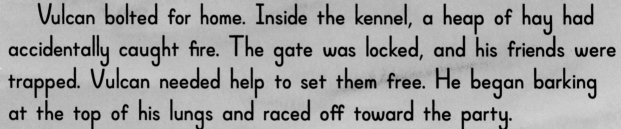

Vulcan bolted for home. Inside the kennel, a heap of hay had accidentally caught fire. The gate was locked, and his friends were trapped. Vulcan needed help to set them free. He began barking at the top of his lungs and raced off toward the party.

One by one, the menagerie heard Vulcan and joined the chorus. Out in the pasture, old Duke bellowed in full voice. Nelson whinnied inside the stables. Royal Gift and Knight of Malta launched into their loudest "hee-haws" and kicked their stalls. Pilot and Gunner woofed wildly. Sweetlips, Captain, and Madam Moose carried the alarm to the mansion's front steps.

The kennel fire occurred in 1792.

The house pets got the message and began disrupting the party. Cockatoo screeched and flew figure-eights over the guests' heads. Parrot perched on the mantle and squawked every word he'd refused to learn from Nelly earlier that day. Pompey and Frisk leaped from one lap to another, while the terriers nipped at everyone's ankles. There was chaos and confusion everywhere, but neither Mount Vernon's family nor any of the party guests understood the danger.

Then, from the front lawn, came a strange and eerie sound no one had ever heard before. It was like the caterwauling of an out-of-tune trombone—a sudden, tremendous, melancholy blast. The eagerly awaited guest had arrived and was lending its powerful voice to the cause.

Everyone rushed outside. Vulcan pointed to the fire. Lucy and Nathan grabbed pots from the kitchen. Sweetlips, Captain, and Madam Moose rounded up the fire buckets. Gunner, Pilot, and Tom Davis came running with pails from the stables. Everyone arrived at the kennel just as Duke came barreling out of the field with a full head of steam and his horns down. He battered through the kennel wall, sending fence posts and rails flying right and left.

In 1785 George Washington listed four *oxen* in his diary, describing one of them—Duke—as "very old" with red brindle markings.

Vulcan dashed into the kennel. "Follow me out!" he barked in his loudest voice. "Drop down, and crawl close to the ground."

With Vulcan's help, the dogs scrambled beneath the smoke and out through the opening Duke had made—each one escaping, safe and sound.

After the fire was out, everyone praised Vulcan for being so brave. Even Lucy and Nathan forgave him for stealing their ham. Vulcan knew he hadn't acted alone. Everyone had worked together to put out the fire, even the mystery guest, who was seen sucking water from the creek and spewing it on the flames.

Vulcan looked around. Standing between Duke and the donkeys was a curious-looking creature. It had funny-looking toes with knobby knees and a scraggly beard under its chin. Its ears were small. Its lips were large, and there was a huge hump in the middle of its back.

"Excusez-moi," Vulcan said to the unusual animal. "My name is Vulcan, and everyone has been anxious to meet you. Please tell us who—and what—are you? And where are you from?"

"I'm a dromedary," answered the tall and dignified guest. "Which is a fancy word for camel. My name is Aladdin, and I come all the way from Arabia."

"Pleased to meet you, Aladdin," said Vulcan. "Welcome to Mount Vernon."

For a Christmas gathering in 1787, General Washington paid a traveling showman to bring a camel to Mount Vernon.

Pompey interrupted the celebration. "Something's wrong with Mopsey!" he shouted. "She's in the General's study."

The animals ran to the mansion. Vulcan and Sweetlips rushed into the house with Pompey while the others crowded outside and peered anxiously through the windows. What they saw made them smile. Mopsey was lying under the General's desk, looking a little less plump and quite satisfied.

George Washington recorded the birth of the foxhound *Mopsey's* litter of eight healthy puppies in his diary in 1768.

She was surrounded by her brand-new litter of eight little puppies.

The hour was late. Everyone was more than ready for a good night's sleep, especially Vulcan. Yet instead of bedding down, they stayed up for hours, watching the new puppies and enjoying one another's company.

Then, off in the distance, they heard . . .

"Got-a-lot-to-do! Got-a-lot-to-do!"
And with that, another day dawned
at Mount Vernon.

The End

Acknowledgments

We would like to express our gratitude to the Mount Vernon Ladies' Association for championing this book. Thanks also go to Stephen McLeod for his calm, capable direction throughout the publication process and to Mary V. Thompson for her meticulous attention to historical accuracy. We are especially indebted to Myra MacPherson for her generous editorial guidance and to Lynn Gammill, Vice Regent for Mississippi of the Mount Vernon Ladies' Association from 1991 to 2011, who was convinced of the story's value and made sure it found its way into print.

—L. B. and M. D.